This Little Tiger book belongs to:

_____

_____

MIKE

FALLS

UP

To Matthew and Georgia on the other side of the world
– CG

To Guillem and Paloma. You make me very happy.
– CB

STRIPES PUBLISHING LIMITED
An imprint of the Little Tiger Group
1 Coda Studios, 189 Munster Road, London SW6 6AW

Imported into the EEA by Penguin Random House Ireland,
Morrison Chambers, 32 Nassau Street, Dublin D02 YH68

First published in Great Britain in 2022

Text copyright © Candy Gourlay, 2022
Illustrations © Carles Ballesteros, 2022

ISBN: 978-1-78895-165-4

The right of Candy Gourlay and Carles Ballesteros to be identified as
the author and illustrator of this work respectively has been asserted
by them in accordance with the Copyright, Designs and Patents Act, 1988.

MIKE

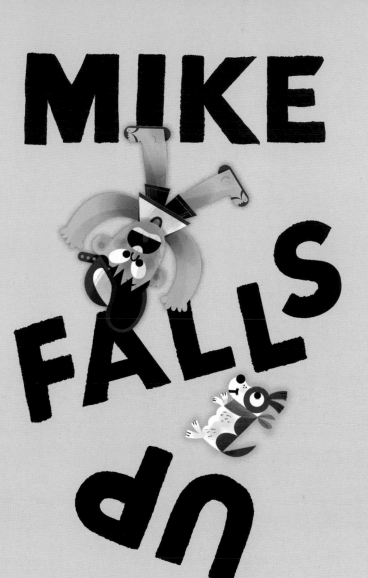

FALLS

UP

Candy Gourlay

Illustrated by Carles Ballesteros

LiTTLE TiGER
LONDON

CHAPTER 1

"It's TOO HOT!"

Mike flopped into a chair. "Too hot to play ... too hot to move ... too hot to do anything!"

Indeed, not a single bird fluttered in the blue sky. Bowow was lying in the shadows under the kitchen table. It was so hot he barely wagged his tail. Even the banana trees in the garden stood absolutely still.

But Mama would have none of it.
She flapped her dishrag at Mike.

"Out, out!" she cried. "Get some fresh air.
And take that dog with you! I will come
and get you when dinner is ready."

She dragged Bowow from under the
table and pushed Mike out the door.

There were thousands of hills around Mike's house, jutting out of the trees and rice paddies. In the rainy season, the mounds were covered in lush green grass.

But in the hot season, the grass was brown as chocolate. That's why they were called the Chocolate Hills.

Mike loved imagining that the hills were scoops of ice cream that a giant had dropped on the landscape by mistake.

If only they really were scoops of ice cream, he thought.

Mike sighed. "Come on, Bowow, let's go up a hill."

"Bow-wow." Bowow didn't sound enthusiastic at all.

At the top it was even hotter. Bowow slumped to the ground, panting. Mike stared at the rice paddies below. He could see the tempting blue stripe of the sea in the distance. So cool but so far away!

Suddenly the ground beneath Mike's flip flops began to tremble.

A crack appeared, zig-zagging between his feet.

"Earthquake!" he cried.

The crack yawned wider, turning into a great hole. Then, as quickly as it had begun, the trembling stopped.

"Bowow, let's get out of here!"

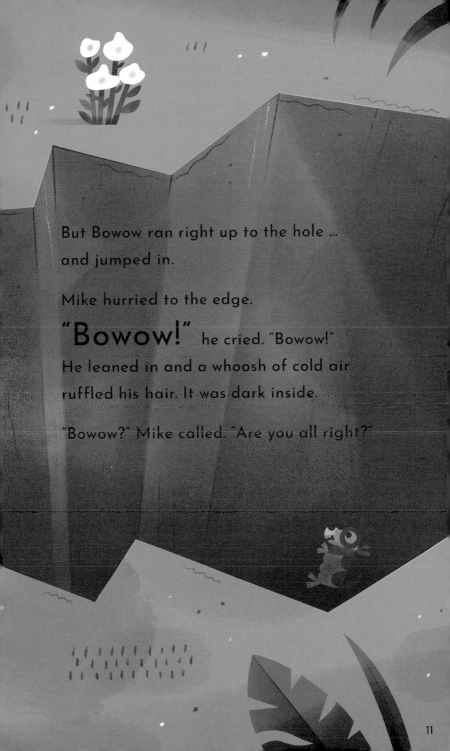

But Bowow ran right up to the hole ...
and jumped in.

Mike hurried to the edge.

"Bowow!" he cried. "Bowow!"
He leaned in and a whoosh of cold air
ruffled his hair. It was dark inside.

"Bowow?" Mike called. "Are you all right?"

Thwack!

Something blew on to his face.

Mike peeled it off. It was a piece of paper.

Written on it in black marker was:

BIRTHDAY.

COME NOW.

JUST FALL UP.

Birthday? Whose birthday?

Just fall up. How was it possible to fall up?

Mike turned it over. It wasn't signed.

Then he heard barking.

Bowow! He sounded a long way away ... but at least he was all right.

Mike stuffed the invite into his pocket and jumped into the hole.

"BOWOW!" he yelled as he tumbled head over heels in the dark. "Where are you?"

"Bow-wow-wow-wow!"

The barking was getting louder!
Mike braced himself for a landing.

But then...

"Bow-wow-wow-wow!"

"Bow-wow-wow-wow!"

"Bow-wow-wow-wow!"

"Bow-wow-wow-wow!"

The barking
faded away.
Had he passed
Bowow?

17

Minutes ticked by and still he was falling -
Mike couldn't tell which way was down or up.

He remembered the message. *Just fall up.*
He was falling up? But which way was *UP*?

Cold air spiralled around him, blowing his
hair about. The rushing air, the darkness -
it was ... relaxing.

He yawned.
"Wake up!"
he told himself crossly.

"Think of
Bowow!"

But he couldn't stop his
eyes drooping ...
and moments later
he was fast asleep.

CHAPTER 2

"Woof!"

Mike's eyes flew open as a tongue
licked him from chin to forehead.

"Urgh!" he cried. "Get off, Bowow! You'll
never believe the dream I just had.
There was an earthquake and ... and—"

"Woof!"

A cold, wet black nose was pressed
against his. Brown doggy eyes
looked at him from behind ringlets
of white hair. The tongue whipped
out again and lathered him from
chin to forehead. Fluffy paws
pressed against his chest.

It was not Bowow. The tongue belonged
to a curly white dog. Mike looked
around. He was lying on a squashy
green beanbag.

"Foofoo!" a voice demanded.
"Is he awake?"

"Woof!" barked the dog.

"About time!" The voice was coming from
behind a pair of bright red glasses.

"Who?" Mike stuttered. "Where?"

"Who? My name is Kaneisha and this is
my dog, Foofoo," the red glasses huffed.
"Where?

MY FIREPLACE.

How dare you whoosh out of
my fireplace like that!"

"Whooshed?" Mike sat up,
suddenly wide awake. "Fireplace?"

There was, indeed, a fireplace in the wall.

Mike had never seen a fireplace before.
It was much too hot for fireplaces
in the Chocolate Hills.

He looked out of the window
over Kaneisha's shoulder.

There was no sign of the Chocolate Hills
or the rice paddies or the blue sky.

There were only tall brick buildings.
And tufts of white blowing around.

It looked like ...

snow.

"But I was in the Chocolate Hills a few minutes ago!" Mike cried. "Where am I now?"

Kaneisha turned and grabbed a thick book from a shelf. She frowned as she flipped through the pages.

"AHA!" She slammed the book shut and hurried over to a small table to consult a plastic globe.

After a few moments, she pointed at a spot on one side of the globe. "This is where your Chocolate Hills are." She spun the globe round and pointed to another spot. "And this is where we are now."

"And where is that?"

"London."

"London!" Suddenly Mike felt very cold. "But how—"

"What is your name?" Kaneisha interrupted.

"Mike..." He was about to tell her about the earthquake and Bowow and the hole when he spotted a piece of paper on the table. He recognized the big marker pen letters at once.

"Hang on!" he said, pointing at the invite.

But before he could explain, the fireplace suddenly made a creaking noise.

"Stand aside!" Kaneisha yelled.
"It might squirt out another boy!"

Mike jumped back. But instead of
a boy, a piece of paper wafted
out of the fireplace.

Foofoo caught it in her mouth and
delivered it to Kaneisha. She held
it up for Mike to see.

Mike pulled his invitation from his
pocket and showed it to Kaneisha.

"You've got one too!" she gasped. "Do you know who's been sending these messages?"

"No, I don't!" Mike told her about the earthquake and the hole in the ground. "My dog Bowow jumped in and I jumped in after him and now I'm here!"

BIRTHDAY. COME NOW. JUST FALL UP.

"My Foofoo would never jump into a strange hole," said Kaneisha.

But as the words left her mouth, Foofoo raced straight for the fireplace.

"No, Foofoo!" Kaneisha cried.

"Stop!"

BIRTHDAY.
COME NOW.
JUST FALL UP.

HURRY
UP.

There was a great gust of wind and –
whoosh! – the curly white dog disappeared.

Then, from inside the chimney,
they heard barking.

"Bow-wow-wow-wow!"

"Woof! Woof! Woof!"

"Bowow!" Mike cried.

"Foofoo!" Kaneisha yelled.

Mike charged into the fireplace.
Instantly he felt a rush of air ... and then
he was falling. Not down though.
He was definitely falling

UP!

Up
the
chimney.

"Foofoo!" a voice yelled behind him.
"Here, girl!"

He looked over
his shoulder.

Kaneisha had kicked off
her fluffy slippers and
jumped in after him.

The barking was much closer now.

"Woof! Woof!"

"Bow-wow-wow-wow!"

"Woof! Woof!"

Mike found his eyelids drooping. "Are you sleepy too?" he asked Kaneisha, yawning.

Zzzzzz.

Kaneisha was snoring.

CHAPTER 3

"Bow-wow-wow-wow!"

A tongue slurped
over his nose and
Mike woke with
a start.

"Bowow!"

Mike threw his arms around his dog. "Bowow! I've found you! You won't believe the dream I've been having. There was a girl with red glasses—"

A face pushed into his. It was wearing red glasses.

"RUN!"

Kaneisha yelled.

Mike ran.

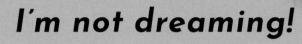

I'm not dreaming!

he thought as he raced after
Kaneisha.

"Kaneisha!" Mike panted.

"Why are we running?"

He looked around. At first he thought they were running between trees. But then he realized they were chimneys made of pink rocks. The ground beneath their feet was weirdly bouncy. Every now and then they passed blocky brown boulders that looked a lot like chocolate cake. Then he saw it...

Rolling right behind them was a ball
of rock. It was huge - maybe a
hundred Bowows tall!

Suddenly the rock ball bounced into the
air and sprouted skinny legs with great
flat feet. Now it was running!

And it was making a strange noise.

"Hee-hee-hee!"

"Does that sound like giggling to you?" Mike called to Kaneisha.

But Kaneisha just screamed **"Monster!"** and ran even faster.

Then the monster opened its mouth and roared.

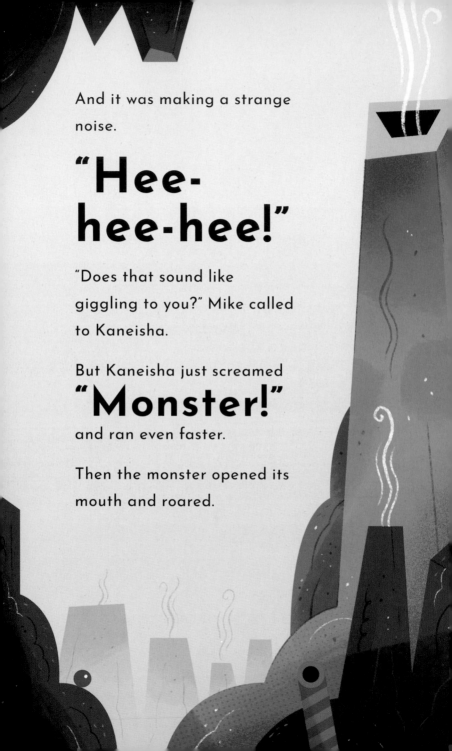

"Woof!"

Foofoo barked.

"Bow-wow-wow!"

Bowow wagged his tail.

Kaneisha grabbed Mike's hand.
"This way!" she cried, zig-zagging
through a narrow gap.

The monster made its giggling noise again.

"Hee-hee-hee!"

Suddenly it clapped its stony hands
over its eyes.

"ONE!"

it shouted in a loud but squeaky voice.

"It's counting," Kaneisha muttered.
"Why is it counting?"

"TWO!"

the monster called.

The counting made the dogs leap
about in excitement.

"THREE!"

"READY OR NOT, HERE I COME!"

"I said... 'Ready or not, here I come!'" the monster called in a small, disappointed voice.

Mike and Kaneisha exchanged glances.

"Er ... are we playing hide and seek now?" Mike asked the monster.

"Play with me!"

Tears began to roll down the monster's face.

Kaneisha peered at the monster.
"You want to play?"

Suddenly the rock monster threw itself
on its back. The ground shook.

"What is it doing?" Kaneisha asked.

"WAAAAAAAH!"

the monster wailed.

It banged its heels on the ground. With
each bang, everyone bounced up and down.

Bounce-bounce-bounce
went Kaneisha and Mike.

"Woof! Woof! Woof!" barked Foofoo.

"Bow-wow-wow-wow!" barked Bowow.

Mike felt something welling up inside his throat. He clamped his mouth shut.

"What's the matter?" Kaneisha said. "You look like you've swallowed a balloon!"

Mike couldn't hold it in any longer. He began to laugh.

At first Kaneisha stared at him but soon she began to laugh too.

The monster had been large and scary and loud. But right now? It looked like a big baby having a tantrum.

Hearing them laugh, the monster stopped wailing and stood up. A big, hopeful smile spread across its rocky face.

Kaneisha and Mike crept out from behind the stone chimneys, smiling.

"So it was you who sent us those messages?" Mike said.

"YES!" The monster nodded vigorously and thumped its feet on the ground in a funny little dance.

"It's
my
birthday!"

"Happy birthday!" Mike and Kaneisha said together.

"Woof! Woof!" barked Foofoo.

"Bow-wow!" barked Bowow.

The monster grinned and began to hop
up and down.

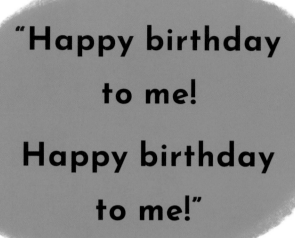

"Happy birthday to me! Happy birthday to me!"

Its hopping sent Mike, Kaneisha and the two dogs flying. But they didn't mind.

It was fun landing on the bouncy ground.
Soon they joined the monster in its

happy dance!

CHAPTER 4

For the next few hours Mike and Kaneisha
played with their new friend.

First they had a game of hide and seek.

Then they played Pass the Puppy, which is a bit like Pass the Parcel - but with dogs.

And finally they joined in with Rock Monster's Footsteps, which is a lot like Grandmother's Footsteps.

It turned out that the boxy boulders that looked like chocolate cake really were made of chocolate cake!

They each had a big slice.

Delicious!

"Happy birthday to you!
Happy birthday to you!
Happy birthday, dear Monster!
Happy birthday to you!"
Mike and Kaneisha sang. The
monster clapped its rocky hands.

They were about to play Pass
the Puppy again when Kaneisha
suddenly remembered... "I've got
homework! I've got to go!"

Uh-oh, Mike thought.
The Chocolate Hills. Mama.
Dinner.

The monster looked sad.

But then it smiled bravely and led Kaneisha and Foofoo to one of the rock chimneys. At the bottom of the chimney was a hole like a fireplace.

"JUST FALL UP," the rock monster told Kaneisha.

"Thanks for having me!" said Kaneisha.
The monster leaned down, wrapped its
arms around Kaneisha and gave her a
gentle squeeze.

Kaneisha ran to Mike and gave him a hug
too. "You can squirt out of my fireplace
anytime," she said. "I don't mind really."

Mike grinned. "Maybe we'll come next week!"

Kaneisha and Foofoo hopped into the rock chimney.

There was a **whoosh** ... and they were gone.

"I have to go home too, Monster," Mike said. "My mama will be looking for me."

The monster nodded.

"Hey, I don't want to call you Monster any more. You're not a monster at all. How about we call you

Rocky?"

Rocky laughed and jumped in delight, sending Mike flying right into a chocolate-cake boulder.

Bowow seemed to approve too. He raced around Rocky barking, "Bow-wow-wow!"

After they ate a little bit more cake,
Rocky showed Mike another rock chimney.

"Come back soon?"

"I'd love to!" Mike smiled as he hopped
into the chimney with Bowow.

A second later they were falling...

Mike woke up and rubbed his eyes.

He was lying on his back, on top of a small hill.

The blue sky was high above his head.

There was a very heavy, very furry, very warm dog lying on top of his belly. Bowow.

It was hot.

Too hot.

He sat up, making Bowow slide
on to the grass.

The Chocolate Hills undulated around
him in great, brown lumpy scoops.

"Mike!"

Mama was standing at the foot of the
hill, shading her eyes from the glare of
the sun.

"Dinner is ready!"

Mike blinked. But hadn't dinner time been and gone? He and Kaneisha had played with Rocky for hours!

Maybe he had dreamed it all. Dreamed about falling to London. Dreamed of meeting a rock monster. Dreamed of the magical birthday party.

But the hill was still cracked. The hole was still there.

At that moment there was a tiny tremble and a cold gust of air blew from the hole.

Mike kneeled down and peered in.

Splat!

A piece of paper hit him in the face.

He pulled it off.

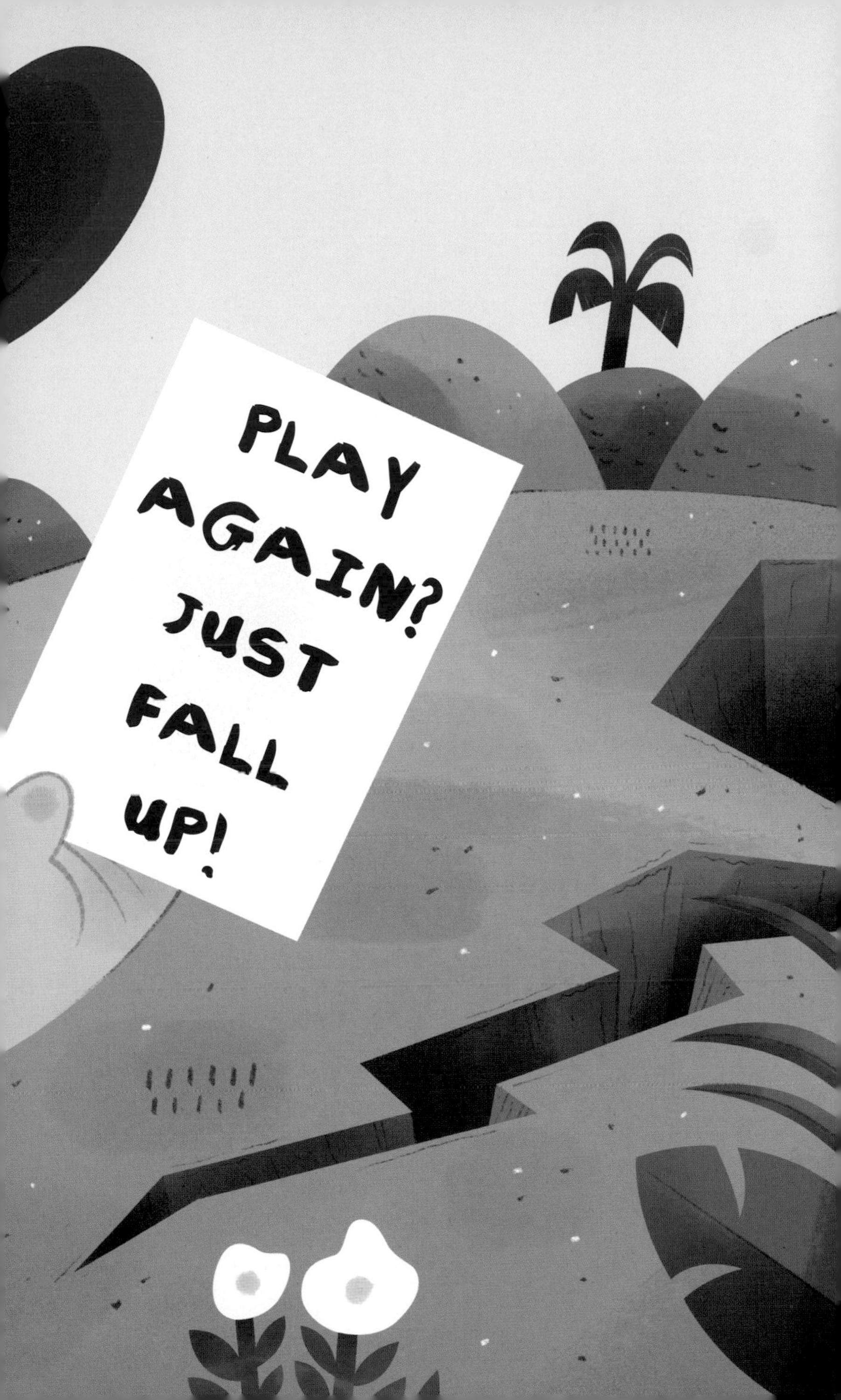
PLAY AGAIN? JUST FALL UP!

COLLECTIBLE STORIES
WITH COLOUR ILLUSTRATIONS